D0116463

Harrison, Paul, 1969-
The elves help Puss in
Boots /
[2017]
33305237838598
ca   05/10/17

TALE MIX-UPS

The Elves
Help
Puss In Boots

written by Paul Harrison
illustrated by Tim Sutcliffe

capstone

2

Once upon a time, there was a cat named Puss In Boots. His master, Jack, fell in love with a princess. Puss defeated an **ogre** so Jack could have the ogre's castle. Then Jack married the princess.

Everyone was very happy. Everyone except Puss. His wonderful boots were worn out. They needed to be fixed.

4

Puss went to
the **cobbler** in the
nearest town.

"Can you fix my
wonderful boots?"
he asked.

"They are wonderful boots, but I'm
afraid I can't fix them," the cobbler
replied. "They are too small and fine
for my big hands."

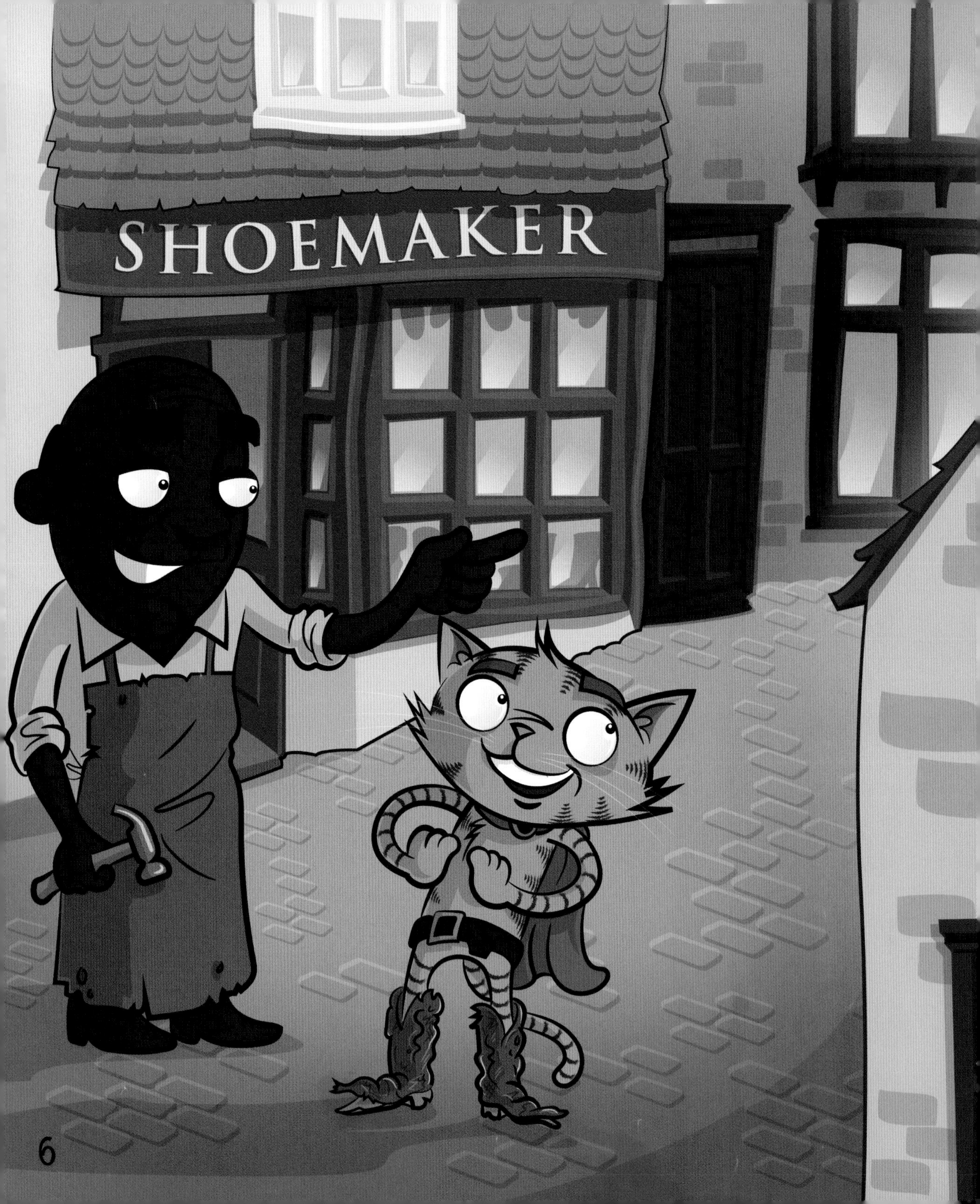
SHOEMAKER

Puss went to the next town and the next, but the **cobblers** always told him the same thing.

Finally one cobbler said, "Boots that wonderful must have been made by fairy folk. I heard there's a shoemaker in the next town who has elves working for him."

Puss ran to the town as fast as his legs would carry him. When he arrived, he stopped in front of the shoemaker's shop. He couldn't believe how lovely the shoes in the window were. He walked inside and showed his boots to the shoemaker.

"Ah, *fairy boots!*" he said. "Yes, I can *fix* them. Come back tonight, and you can watch."

That night, Puss returned to the shoemaker's shop. Puss and the shoemaker hid in a closet so the elves wouldn't see them. They peeked through the gap in the door and waited.

As the clock struck **midnight**, two elves appeared dressed in rags.

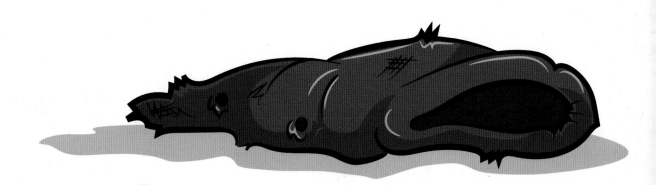

Puss watched as the elves worked.
In no time at all, his boots were fixed.
Then the elves disappeared into the
night. The boots looked as good as
new—better even!

Puss was overjoyed.
But the shoemaker
was not.

"What's the matter?" asked Puss.

"I want to **reward** the elves," said the shoemaker. "But they have no use for money. I thought I might make them new clothes instead. But I can't find a thread that is strong yet fine enough to use."

It was true. The elves deserved something for all their hard work. Puss thought long and hard. Where could they find thread that would do the job?

He scratched his whiskers. That was it! His whiskers would work perfectly!

Puss plucked out a couple of whiskers and gave them to the shoemaker. The shoemaker went to work right away.

That night they set out the new clothes for the elves. Then they both waited for the clock to strike **midnight**.

When the elves saw the clothes, they jumped around the room with joy. Puss had saved the day!

Puss In Boots

The *Puss In Boots* story that is well known was written by French writer Charles Perrault in 1697. In this story, Puss belongs to a miller's son. The miller's son is poor, but Puss is clever. Puss catches rabbits and other animals to give to the king. The cat pretends they are gifts from his master, who Puss says is a rich young man. Puss then defeats an **ogre** so the miller's son can live in the ogre's castle. The king is impressed with the gifts and the castle. The miller's son marries the king's daughter.

The Elves and the Shoemaker

This story comes from two German brothers named Jacob and Wilhelm Grimm. They collected fairy tales from Europe during the 1800s. In this story, a poor shoemaker has only one piece of leather left to make shoes. He goes to bed and wakes up to find that elves have turned the leather into a pair of beautiful shoes. The elves, who are dressed in rags, come back each night to make more shoes. The shoemaker becomes rich. To thank the elves, he makes them new clothes. The elves are overjoyed.

Glossary

cobbler—someone who fixes shoes

midnight—twelve o'clock at night

ogre—a monster or giant who eats people

reward—to give a gift or award for doing something good

Writing Prompts

Write a thank-you letter from the elves to the shoemaker. What do you think they liked most about their new clothes?

Can you retell the story from the cobbler's point of view? How pleased do you think he was when Puss came up with his great idea?

Imagine you were hiding in the closet with Puss and the shoemaker. Describe what it would be like waiting for the elves to come. What could you see at midnight?

Read More

McFadden, Deanna. *The Elves and the Shoemaker* (Silver Penny Stories). New York: Sterling Children's Books, 2012

Perrault, Charles and Arthur, Malcolm. *Puss in Boots*. New York: Square Fish, 2011

Pinkney, Jerry. *Puss in Boots*. New York: Dial Books, 2012

The Elves and the Shoemaker. New York: Parragon Books, 2013

Internet Sites

Facthound offers a safe, fun way to find websites related to this book. All the sites on Facthound have been researched by our staff.

Here's all you do:
Visit **www.facthound.com**
Type in this code: 9781410983039

Read all the books in the series:

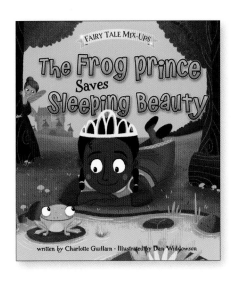

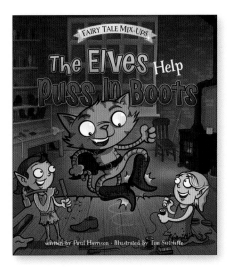

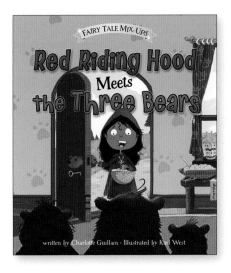

Visit www.mycapstone.com

© 2017 Raintree
an imprint of Capstone Global Library, LLC
Chicago, Illinois

To contact Capstone Global Library please call 800-747-4992, or visit our website www.capstonepub.com

All rights reserved. No part of this publication may be reproduced or transmitted in any form or by any means, electronic or mechanical, including photocopying, recording, taping, or any information storage and retrieval system, without permission in writing from the publisher.

Edited by Penny West
Designed by Steve Mead
Original illustrations © Capstone Global Library Ltd 2016
Illustrated by Tim Sutcliffe, Inky Illustration Agency
Production by Steve Walker
Originated by Capstone Global Library Limited

20 19 18 17 16
10 9 8 7 6 5 4 3 2 1

Library of Congress Cataloging-in-Publication data is available on the Library of Congress website.

ISBN: 978-1-4109-8303-9 (library binding)
ISBN: 978-1-4109-8311-4 (paperback)
ISBN: 978-1-4109-8315-2 (eBook PDF)

Summary: Puss thinks no one can fix his boots. But there's a shoemaker in a far off town who has an unusual way of fixing shoes.

Every effort has been made to contact copyright holders of any material reproduced in this book. Any omissions will be rectified in subsequent printings if notice is given to the publisher.

All the Internet addresses (URLs) given in this book were valid at the time of going to press. However, due to the dynamic nature of the Internet, some addresses may have changed, or sites may have changed or ceased to exist since publication. While the author and publisher regret any inconvenience this may cause readers, no responsibility for any such changes can be accepted by either the author or the publisher.

Printed and bound in China
PO007731LEOF16